The Phantom of Billy Bantam

The Phantom of Billy Bantam

Penny Dolan

illustrated by Philip Hopman

To Gabrielle, Phil, Emily and Hannah
with much love.

This edition produced for the Book People Ltd,
Hall Wood Avenue, Haydock, St Helens WA11 9UL

First published by Scholastic Ltd, 2004
This edition published by Scholastic Ltd, 2005

Text copyright © Penny Dolan, 2004
Illustrations copyright © Philip Hopman, 2004
Cover illustration copyright © Klaas Verplancke, 2004

ISBN 0 439 95565 3

Printed and bound by Nørhaven Paperback A/S, Denmark

The right of Penny Dolan and Philip Hopman to be identified as the author
and illustrator of this work respectively has been asserted by them in accordance
with the Copyright, Designs and Patents Act, 1988.

Chapter One

Now and again, as he flickered through the reeds, he'd see them – the living – and start to hope again. But they turned away in fear, whispering, "It's Billy Bantam! Beware of Billy Bantam!"

Folk named him and blamed him for any ripple of bad luck that flowed through the fens. What happened in the past had been nothing to do with him, but sometimes stories live longer than truth. Occasionally a bitter chill burnt in his lonely heart. He'd tried so hard to be friendly. Perhaps evil would be easier?

Then he saw her, the girl, clambering down from a cart. She had a determined look about her. Would she be the one? Would she trust the phantom of long-lost Billy Bantam?

* * *

All that day, as the cart jolted along, Annie relived what had happened. There was the terrible morning when the rent tin had been too empty to rattle, and the bread-bin held only two dry crusts. There was the awful evening when Mam had seized Annie's hands, and said she was off to work as a cook in a big, grand house. At first, Annie had grinned excitedly, but Mam hadn't smiled back.

"Annie, I can't take you or the little ones with me," she sighed. "I'm sending you to Slodger's Fen."

"Slodger's what? Who? Where?" asked Annie, alarmed.

"Slodger's Fen, where your poor father came from," Mam said, lifting an old carrying case down from the shelf. "Uncle Foskitt and Granny Tidd have sent word you can stay."

"Uncle Foskitt? Granny Tidd? But I've never seen them, Mam," protested Annie.

"They've seen you, my pet. It's where you were born," Mam answered, "so I know you'll be welcome at Tidd Cottage."

Soon, there they were, sitting on the brewer's cart. Four-year-old Tilly was tucked tightly by Annie's side. The twins, Josh and Joe, wriggled excitedly, and admired their newly mended boots. Mam slipped a plump twist of paper into Annie's pocket, and stood back from the cart's wheels.

The horses snorted, and shook their manes. Then, steadily, they stepped forward, and the cart was on its way.

"Tell Granny Tidd I'll come when I can," Mam called, waving. "Take care of them, Annie!"

* * *

Now, at last, the horses halted at a sturdy
stone bridge. The main road led over that
bridge, and on to some unseen town, but the
children were getting off here.

As Annie clambered down, she smelt salt,
and water, and wildness on the wind.

Determinedly she looked around. Near the
bridge was a twisted stile, and beyond it,
the flat, misty marshes of Slodger's Fen
stretching away towards the far-off sea.
The reed beds seemed to go on for ever.
Nobody was there to meet them.

The kindly carter lifted the young ones
down from his wagon, and they stood close
to their big, brave sister. Annie wasn't
feeling very brave, but Mam had told her
what to do.

"If Uncle Foskitt isn't there, take the narrow path that leads straight from the stile. Cross the plank bridge, and when you see the huge stone set in the riverbank, Tidd Cottage will be close by. You'll need to look hard, as it's not easily found."

The carter shuffled his feet, and looked up at the sky. It was already late afternoon.

"Please go," Annie insisted, "I know the way from here. Thank you so much."

"If you're certain, miss," the carter agreed, anxious to get on his way.

"I am," Annie said, as cheerfully as she could. She didn't want the little ones to worry.

The carter handed down the last bundle, and leant close to her ear. "Take care, miss, as you're stepping across Slodger's Fen," he murmured. "It's a strange, tricksy place, and there's odd folk hereabouts. Very odd folk indeed."

He shook the reins, the horses plodded onwards, and the cart disappeared into the distance, on its way to the next town.

Chapter Two

Annie gave one bundle to Josh, one to Joe, and grabbed little Tilly's hand tightly.

"We'll follow the path, like Mam told me," she said, "but keep away from the water, do you hear me?"

Annie shepherded them along the soft, peaty path. The dark river lapped the steep, slippery banks of Deepwater Cut beside them, and waterfowl called unseen in the tall reeds.

They had already
lost sight of the road
when Annie saw a
strange, pale boy
watching them from
the far bank. He was
half-hidden by the
tall rushes, and
seemed to move
along as she moved.

She smiled at him, in as friendly a way as
she could manage, but he didn't smile back.
Maybe he was one of the odd folk she'd
been warned about? Next time Annie
glanced across, he'd disappeared. A small
shiver ran down her back.

Soon she had other troubles. Little Tilly
sank down on to the path, and began to
cry. "Too far!" she grizzled, kicking her
heels. "Can't, can't, can't!" Josh and Joe
were struggling with their bundles, and
biting back tears too.

Annie forced herself to give a big smile, and fumbled under her shawl. She found Mam's plump twist of paper in her pocket, and fished out three round toffee-drops. She held the sweets on her palm. "Will these help you go a bit further?" Tilly scrambled to her feet. The boys beamed, and reached out.

"Suck slowly. They're as hard as bullets," Annie warned, shoving the rest of the sweets back in her pocket. She dared not let the little ones rest for long. "Come on. It won't be far."

Salty wind raced along the ditches and streams. Tall reeds twisted and danced. Hidden creatures darted from the banks, and dived into the depths. It seemed an utter wilderness.

"Don't turn off that path, my girl, or you'll never find your way back," Mam had warned. "And don't let those babies slip into Deepwater Cut, or they'll be swept out to sea. Take care, Annie, take care." Annie felt tears push into her eyes.

Now, far off, she saw the thin thread of the sea-bank – and a peculiar house. From here it seemed as small as a thimble, and the flag on the roof flapped like a minute crow. A window glinted, like an eye watching everything around. Annie was glad they weren't going there. She hurried on, into the early dusk.

At last they came to a rickety wooden bridge, set across a wide ditch. The well-worn boards sat on sturdy posts, and there was one thin wooden railing as a handhold. This must be the plank bridge, thought Annie. "We'll be there soon!" she said with a smile.

Just then two dark, furry faces popped up from the ripples, dived again, and reappeared with whiskery grins. "Look, Annie!" the boys called, laughing.

"Be careful, you two!" she ordered, sternly. "Otters can swim. You can't!"

Bother! That boy was there again, ghostly pale, as if he was trying to speak. What did he want? She didn't have time to stop and chat. Annie edged Josh and Joe and Tilly carefully up on to the narrow bridge. The water was dark and deep below, and the boys started counting the darting fishes.

Billy Bantam watched from the rushes. He watched the girl, the one that had smiled at him, and the little ones who laughed and chatted happily. He longed to be as happy as they were. Just then he heard the faintest of sounds. What was it? Water was starting to swish and gurgle and swell and surge, and at once he knew that something was moving upstream, making the river level rise, as once the flood had swelled around him – and it was coming this way.

"Shall I warn her?" Billy wondered. "Yes? No?" He sighed. Would this girl be any different to the rest? Would she blame him for bringing the danger too?

Billy gathered his spirit together, and
appeared again, just beyond the bridge.
Annie gasped as she saw his pale, ghostly
face. Then she heard a voice that must have
been his, ringing in her head.

"Hold on as tight as you can. Don't let go!
There's a rush of water coming, but you'll be
safe if you hold tight, tight, tight..."

"Hold tight!" Annie screamed to the boys,
grabbing at Tilly as fast as she could. "Hold
on as tight as you can! Whatever you do,
don't let go!"

They seized the handrail. The long green weeds writhed below the bridge, and all of a sudden a wave of water rose up around them. It surged right over the wobbling planks, and washed right over their ankles.

Annie saw something long and large and silvery slide beneath them, and away along the stream. Just as swiftly, the water dropped back to its old level, leaving them half-drenched, but safe.

The twins' panic gave way to giggles as they saw how wet their feet were. "Naughty river!" said Tilly crossly, and that made them all laugh. Relieved, Annie edged them back on to dry land. They weren't as scared as she was, it seemed.

She looked for that weird boy again, but he had gone. Doubt hit her. How had he known about the creature that nearly tipped them into the water? Had he sent it? Had he tried to drown them?

Away over the reeds, Annie saw the dark sail of a boat.

"Where are you, you slimy monster?" came a rough voice rising in rage. "No one escapes from Captain Slew! I'll have you back in my clutches soon enough!"

Annie hurried down the path. She shut her mind to the ghostly boy and the vicious voice, and strode on as briskly as she could with the little ones, whistling loudly to show she was not afraid.

Chapter Three

Then Annie heard someone whistling in reply.

"Hello! Hello!" Joe and Josh shouted,
sending a flock of birds flapping into the air.

A tall, thin man appeared on the path.
As he lurched towards them, they saw he
had a wooden crutch under one arm, and
a bandage pinned around one knee, but
he waved a huge hand in a cheery greeting.

"Hello, my dearies!" he called, "Hello, my poppets! 'Tis I, your Uncle Foskitt!"

They liked him at once. They liked his wrinkled, weather-worn face beaming below his strange leathery cap. They liked his lolloping waterproof boots, and the way his elbows stuck out of his flapping leathery jacket. He shook their hands, apologized for not being there to meet the cart, and then led them on.

"What happened to your leg, Uncle Foskitt?" asked Josh and Joe.

"Harrrummph!" he snorted, limping along. "My leg got into a bad argument with Captain Slew and his blasted dinghies."

"Who's Slew? Who's Slew?" squealed the boys, giggling. "Who's Slew?"

Annie stayed silent. It was Slew she had heard on that dark-sailed ship.

"'Tis no laughing matter, young 'uns," said Uncle Foskitt, scowling. "He's a big bully, that's what he is. See over there?" Foskitt pointed to the far-off house Annie had noticed earlier. "That precious pimple on the sea wall is Captain Slew's den of thieves," he hissed. "Slew and his gang of pirates are a terrible torment to us water-folk, stealing and grabbing whatever we have." Foskitt eyed the twins severely. "So you two must watch your tiny hides, and do as you're told while you're here!"

The twins went very quiet, and Annie gulped. She decided not to mention the incident at the bridge.

24

"Oh dearie me!" Uncle Foskitt said, and gathered them in a hug. "Don't be too afraid, Annie girl, nor you young 'uns, neither. I only wanted to give a warning. You'll all be safe enough in Tidd Cottage. Slimy Slew ain't found us yet, for all his spying spyglasses."

They had come to a huge stone beside the riverbank. Uncle Foskitt grinned, beckoned with one bony finger, and led them into the reeds. Mam was right. Tidd Cottage was hard to find, and that was because it didn't look like a building at all.

At first glance, it seemed no more than a heap of broken hulls, laying low among the reeds. Old nets, wicker baskets and fish-traps were wedged like barnacles in the crevices. Close by, a heap of drying reeds almost hid a pair of small boats.

Uncle Foskitt bent down, and pushed open a narrow door. "Here they are! Come at last," he cried, grinning widely.

The room was like an overcrowded cabin.

Odd bundles hung from the rafters, or dangled against the walls. A hammock hung from the ceiling. And there, over by an iron stove, was a little old woman, even more wrinkled than Uncle Foskitt. Granny Tidd! She had bright brown eyes, and a quick, mischievous smile. She stood on a stool, stirring a pot of soup.

"Welcome, welcome! Get those wet things off at once," she cried, squinting at their muddy feet, "and sit down, sit down, my chicklings."

She ladled soup swiftly into the bowls on the table, and Uncle Foskitt cut slices of crusty bread. Soon they were slurping hot broth, and were warm and dry again.

Once the little ones were settled soundly in
their bed, Annie paced up and down,
feeling restless. She was missing Mam, and
wanted time to think.

"Please?" she asked. "Can I go outside for
a moment?"

"No further than a step, Annie," said Uncle
Foskitt. "There's strange spirits in these
marshes, my dear."

"Don't worry. She'll keep her eyes open,
will that one," murmured Granny Tidd wisely.
"My old knitting needles sense it. Bolt the
door well when you come in, Annie!"

Annie stood there, watching the silky water flow swiftly towards the sea, and thinking of her mother. Had she ever seen the ghostly boy? She hadn't mentioned him.

All at once Annie heard a call, like a night bird, and a gentle laugh. Annie scanned the water nervously and the boy appeared again, standing across on the opposite bank, pale in the moonlight. Now she saw he was about her age, but thinner. Annie paused. There was something about him that made her uneasy, especially after Uncle Foskitt's warnings, but she wouldn't let it show. And if he was here, he wasn't one of Slew's crew.

"Hello there," she said, her voice echoing across the watery darkness. "It's nice to meet you, whoever you are."

The spectral boy nodded, very slowly, and smiled back, as if he might answer. At that moment a swift breeze set the reeds swaying. He seemed to sway and shimmer too, and then strangely he was gone.

Annie turned, her heart beating anxiously, and hurried back into the ramshackle house. She slid the bolt securely into place. Foskitt was snoring away in his hammock. Granny Tidd was in her rocking chair, huddling a blanket under her chin. The old woman looked across at Annie, and grinned.

"Well, well!" she murmured. "Seems my knitting needles were telling me right. See anyone?"

Annie suddenly felt sure Granny Tidd knew about the mysterious boy. "Who is he?" she asked.

"What you saw was the phantom of poor Billy Bantam, my dear," Granny Tidd answered. "Don't be afraid. I'll tell you his tale tomorrow."

Annie sank into her trundle bed in the corner of the room, but before she had time to puzzle over poor Billy, she fell fast asleep.

Chapter Four

Next morning the boys kept squabbling over who saw the otters first. Eventually Uncle Foskitt looked up from where he was working on the nets and lines.

"Maybe, if you watch out for Slew, you could take the boys down to the plank bridge when the mist's cleared?"

Annie nodded. Josh and Joe were fussing about with an old glass bottle now, and scribbling on a scrap of paper. They had charcoal all over their hands. A walk seemed a very good idea.

"Me too?" asked Tilly.

Annie beamed. "You too!"

The otters were there, diving and somersaulting about in the water. Thankfully there was no sign of the boy, or the surging water, though Annie watched all the time. As they turned for home, Annie saw Josh drop the glass bottle in the water.

"What's that?" she asked.

"For Mam," the twins replied, as the bottle
bobbed away on the ripples.

* * *

That evening, when Uncle Foskitt was busy
outside and the little ones were snuggled
up, fast asleep, Annie sat down beside
Granny Tidd.

"Tell me about Billy Bantam, please,
Granny."

To Annie's surprise, Granny looked nervous. "Be watchful when you speak of Billy, especially if Foskitt's near," the old woman whispered. "Some say that Billy's a bringer of trouble, my dear."

Annie shivered, remembering the thing beneath the bridge.

"Well," began Granny Tidd quietly, "when I was younger than you are now, poor Billy was a human boy, all right. He was a small skivvy up at that sea-wall house! Slaved him to the bone, those owners did.

Fed him on scraps and sweepings. They even locked him in the chicken-coop to sleep among the hens and bantams. Passing sailors tried to help, but any kindness made things worse for the lad."

Annie felt sorry for Billy. Her life had been hard, but never cruel.

"He was a cheerful soul, though!" chuckled Granny Tidd. "I'd see him standing on the quay at Deepwater Neck. He was always larking about, singing songs about strange old legends and telling tales of mermaids and sea monsters and storms. He made people listen, whether they liked it or not." The old woman paused, and gave a deep, sad sigh. "Then one night a storm sprang up, a real wrecker, bringing damage on land and sea. Someone said it was his songs that had summoned up the storm, and that set a rumour going, blaming it all on Billy. But nobody got to ask him, though, 'cos Billy was washed away with the waves."

"Lost in the sea?"

Granny Tidd nodded. "But bad words can be stronger than good ones, my girl, so even to this day, some say a curse falls on anyone who sees Billy Bantam."

Annie gasped. "Is it true?"

"What do you think, girl? They're just ignorant fools! Don't you fret about seeing poor Billy," Granny Tidd said, smoothing Annie's hair. "Sssh, now! Foskitt's back!"

The door opened, and in came Uncle Foskitt, looking gaunt and tired. He groaned, and rubbed his sore leg. "It'll be slow work checking my nets tomorrow," he said. "I'm feeling weary tonight, Granny Tidd."

Annie lay in bed that night, thinking. She couldn't bear to see poor Uncle Foskitt in such a state. She wasn't sure how long they'd be at Tidd Cottage. A month? A year? Or longer? Oh no! But surely, while she was here, she could help him – if Granny Tidd minded the little ones? Early next morning she spoke with Granny Tidd. She was delighted. Then she whispered her plan to Joe and Josh and Tilly. Now all she had to do was ask Uncle Foskitt.

* * *

As Uncle Foskitt groaned over his breakfast, Granny Tidd sat there, grinning about Annie's plan. "Go on, Annie," she urged.

"Uncle Foskitt," Annie said, "Granny Tidd's looking after the little ones today. So I can help you, if you want."

"Well, blow me down! My leg feels better already," Uncle Foskitt said, beaming with sudden relief. "I'll be pleased indeed to have company, Annie."

When the meal was over, he dragged his waterproof jacket from the shelf, and pulled out a smaller jacket and a cap for Annie. She tucked her hair inside, away from the wind.

"You looks like a proper water-pup now, my dear," he said, striding towards the river. "We won't be long, Granny, and we'll be careful!"

Granny Tidd nodded at Annie. "Make sure you are, my girl!"

Chapter Five

Annie jumped into the boat, and Uncle Foskitt rowed away, along hidden cuts and narrow creeks.

"I keep my sail down these days," he explained, "well out of Slew's sight."

Uncle Foskitt soon let Annie take one of the oars, and on they rowed together. His nets were hidden in secret pools or below low branches. Sometimes they dragged the little boat over short, peat paths, and set off again in fresher waters.

Later that day they steered into the wider reaches of Deepwater River, but Uncle Foskitt kept the boat in the ruffled reflections of the reeds and rushes.

"Look there, my dear!" he whispered, pointing to the sea wall. "That's Deepwater Neck – and Captain Uglow Slew's horrid headquarters!"

On the quay was the odd house Annie had seen before. It was dirty and foul, and it seemed worse now she knew poor Billy had

lived there too. Did he still haunt this place? The tattered flag flapped madly above the sloping slate roof. Vile shouts and carousings came from inside. Suddenly a huge bearded figure staggered into the doorway and bawled a curse aloud. The light within the den made his shadow spread like a giant across the river.

"Uglow Slew and his horrible crew!" muttered Uncle Foskitt. "Nobbut scurvy pirates, the lot of them, so be warned."

Boats had sailed through Deepwater Neck once, between the two enormous pillars and the lanterns that marked the gap in the sea wall. They were headed for the open sea. Now the waterway was barred, and its lantern lights broken. A vast, ugly raft floated there, blocking the Neck. Annie stared, seeing the spiked gates in the towering tollbooths, and the skeleton hands of wheeled wooden winches ready to catch passing craft.

"Nobody can pass without Slew knowing," spat Uncle Foskitt. "He snatches and snitches our goods, and all our lives are wrecked by his greed. But we'll soon get the better of him, Annie, you just wait and see. And where does this evil come from?" he hissed, "From the home of the Phantom of Billy Bantam! So beware, Annie! Beware of Billy Bantam!"

Uncle Foskitt steered the boat away in haste. Gradually, as they got closer to home, he began to smile again. "I've got a good haul today, Annie, thanks to you," he said, sliding across to the other end of the boat. "Take both oars now, my dearie," he said, "you're doing fine! Row on!"

* * *

Annie soon became a strong rower. As the days went by Uncle Foskitt showed her the hidden ways through the reed-beds, and how to guide the boat into the safest channels. She learnt how the tides tugged away, exposing treacherous mudbanks, and how the salt water surged inland at high tide.

The boys were always waiting for Annie to return. "When can we come with you?" they asked. "Soon," said Annie, telling them about all she'd seen: the fish and the seals and the birds.

"Have you seen the big sea?" they asked.

"I've seen it far away," she answered. She did not tell them about Slew's revolting raft, blocking Deepwater Neck.

With time, Annie began to feel as if an invisible map was growing in her mind, patterned with all the streams and ditches she rowed by day. Soon she dreamt she was rowing those secret ways in her sleep.

Then, one night, a long, silvery shape – a monstrous thing with fronded gills and small eyes – swam through those dream waters. It was the creature she'd seen below the rickety bridge, the thing Slew was trying to recapture. Strangely, she wasn't scared in her dream, for someone was in the boat with her. She couldn't see them because of the mist, but it wasn't Uncle Foskitt.

Whenever Annie leant forward to find out, she'd wake with a start from her haunting dream.

Chapter Six

The next morning Uncle Foskitt hurried
around, collecting various packages together.
Annie didn't have to wait long to find out
what Uncle Foskitt was up to. "Slew won't
stop us water-folk selling our goods," he
chuckled. "There's a cunning plan afoot!"

"And pigs might fly," snapped Granny Tidd
furiously, spitting in the fire. "Don't be a fool,
Foskitt. Have you forgotten Slew's crew gave
you that bad leg? You'd better watch out for

yourself, 'cos he'll be watching out for you. And did you ask if you could go bartering that bundle of my best knitted socks?"

Uncle Foskitt stormed out of Tidd Cottage, dragging Annie with him. He rowed angrily along, down one narrow cut and along another.

"Where are we going?" asked Annie.

"Wait and see!" Uncle Foskitt said, and began to smile.

All at once the narrow cut opened out into a smooth lake, edged by trees. "'Tis Deepwater Mere," said Uncle Foskitt.

Several small craft were roped together around a massive mooring post. It was a floating water market! People moved from boat to boat, opening their baskets and bags, bargaining and bartering. They spoke in whispers. Annie saw the tip of Slew's flag fluttering close by, above the tall reeds. This secret, tree-lined mere was right under Slew's nose. That was why everyone was keeping so quiet!

While Uncle Foskitt traded fish for honey, and socks for sacks of flour, Annie rested over the oars. A grey heron darted swiftly into the glittering lake. When it rose, a fish was wriggling in its sharp beak. Annie shuddered, and thought of Captain Slew, watching the marshlands from his window's glass eye. Who would he pick on next?

Then Annie heard a sound, as if the wind was rising in the reeds. Slowly, the swishing turned to a whispering, and the whispering into words. "Look out, Annie, look out!" It was Billy's voice again, although there was no sign of him.

Annie looked, and saw a glint of sunlight behind a tree stump, like light reflecting from a spyglass. She screwed up her eyes and peered even harder. Yes! Two men were crouching there, spying on the water market.

Then they turned and hurried away. Annie was sure they were from Slew's crew. It wasn't safe to stay at the market any longer.

"Uncle Foskitt," she begged, "We must go. Please! Please row!"

"What a rush you're in, my dearie." Uncle Foskitt stowed his last package away under the seat. "But we'll go home if you want it so, young Annie."

Expertly he took both oars, turned the craft around, and paddled soundlessly away from the Mere. They had not gone very far when a dark sail appeared above the reeds, followed by shouts and the sound of muskets. They heard a chorus of cries from the water-folk, as they tried to escape.

That familiar rough voice bellowed out, sending a thousand birds circling wildly overhead. "You think you can fool me? Don't forget, I spy with my one big eye on all you do, you paltry water-snails!"

Uncle Foskitt cringed. "It's Slew and his wretched ruffians," he said. "We got away just in time, Annie."

Annie sat quietly, thinking. "Thank you, Billy Bantam," she murmured.

"What did you say?" snapped Uncle Foskitt.

"Nothing," she replied swiftly. "Nothing at all."

Josh and Joe were watching the otter cubs slither about in the shallows. As soon as Uncle Foskitt's boat appeared, the boys leapt up.

"Can we come in the boat now?" they asked.

"Not now," said Uncle Foskitt gruffly, clambering up on to the bank. Dejected, the boys went back to the otters, while Uncle Foskitt told Granny Tidd about the market.

Then he slumped down, exhausted, and was soon sleeping as soundly as Tilly.

There was a plate full of comforting scones on the table. Annie tucked in hungrily, deep in thought.

"He warned you, then?" said Granny Tidd, unexpectedly, "Sure as frogs is frogs!"

Annie looked up, startled, then nodded.

"It's not many as can see our phantom Billy, let alone hear his voice. Foskitt can't, for all he knows of the marshes. Sometimes I think that's why Foskitt's so set against him," Granny Tidd added.

But who is right? Annie wondered. Is the Phantom of Billy Bantam truly to be trusted?

* * *

As evening drew on, over at Deepwater Neck the tide slid under Slew's barricade, carrying an old glass bottle. A greasy hand, studded with ruby rings, reached into the water, and snatched the bottle up.

A bloodshot eye peered inside, and a fat finger extracted a crumpled, charcoal grey map. It showed several smudged otter faces, the plank bridge, the huge stone, a tall, thin man and – quite clearly – the hulls that made up Tidd Cottage. Words were scribbled in one corner: *"To Mam. Come soon. Love from Josh and Joe."*

An evil grin spread across Slew's face. He slid the map into his bulging pocket, and dropped the bottle back in the water. "Aha! I'll get you now, Foskitt, so I will."

Chapter Seven

Annie woke as if she'd been called, and peered through the shutters. It was just before dawn, grey and misty. Uncle Foskitt's boat was bobbing in the water – and the pale phantom boy was sitting at the stern. He stared at her, with wide unblinking eyes.

He wants me to go with him, she thought, aghast. She turned away from the window, hesitating. What should she do? She shrugged, grabbed her jacket and crept out of the door.

As if by a spell, the boat moved silently, drifting through the mists that wreathed the trailing willows. Then they swung out into the salty tide. Strands of seaweed floated along in the current, and Slew's barricade appeared ahead.

Annie shivered, hoping the fog was hiding them from view. Just then she had a moment of doubt. Was Billy taking her into the grasp of this evil man? Was he luring her into a trap? The phantom's face was pale and his eyes huge and wild. Billy seemed to be flickering, quivering, but not with fear.

They drew closer. An angry rooster, tethered by one foot, squawked from a chicken-coop on the quay, calling the dawn. Billy turned away, and shuddered. The horror in his pale face made Annie shudder too.

All of a sudden Captain Uglow Slew surged out on to the quay. A putrid smell filled the air. Golden earrings glinted in his ears, and an eyepatch covered one eye.

A tangle of whiskers circled his bloated face. He wore an enormous captain's coat, crusted with tarnished gold, as a dressing-gown. A filthy nightshirt flapped about above his creaking sea-boots.

Coughing at the dawn air, Slew made
his way on to his floating barrier. He held
a vast, steaming cooking pot, wrapped in
a grubby cloth, and ruby carbuncle rings
glittered from his grimy fingers.

Slew tugged at the ropes that anchored
a vast net to the raft, waking whatever was
curled in the net. It began heaving and
writhing about horribly.

"Coochi-coo, my darling!" Uglow's hoarse voice croaked. He spoke as if he was talking to a pet. "Wake up, wake up! Something to build you up, my precious!" Uglow poured foul, stinking porridge out of the pot. Down it glooped, down around the net. The water thrashed and splashed, as if Slew's captive was desperate and angry – and hungry.

"Let me have a look at you then, my 'orrible darling!" Uglow crooned.

A slithery tail flicked out of the foam, and was gone. Annie had seen that tail swirl under the plank bridge, but it was even bigger now. Her hands flew to cover her mouth.

"Eat, my pretty thing, eat," she heard Slew croon. "Eat and grow fat! Then we'll set you on those water-folk, won't we?"

All at once she knew what the creature was. An enormous eel! Slew was making the thing his slave, feeding it until it grew huge enough to keep the water-folk in his power.

The Phantom of Billy Bantam gazed across at Annie. His pale hair fluttered around his head, and his strange eyes glowed. Yes, the girl had been as determined as he had hoped. Now she knew the danger he'd seen Slew brewing for so long. Now someone else could give warning – and be believed! The pain in his heart shifted a little.

The sun was lifting the mist, so it was no longer safe in the Neck. Annie let the incoming tide take the boat inland, and soon they were safely hidden once more. Annie paused as a pair of swans swooped past

 with the morning sun on their wings. Then she turned back to

face the phantom boy. He was gone.

"Bother you, Billy. What am I supposed to do now?" she muttered as she rowed back alone.

At breakfast Annie sat sipping her hot drink.

"Go and watch the otters for a moment," she told the little ones.

"Will you take us in the boat if we do?" said Josh.

"To see the sea?" said Joe.

Annie nodded. "Yes. Soon."

When they were gone, she put down her cup. "I went out –" she said, hesitating – "in the boat early this morning."

"Goosey gracious! All on your own, Annie?" Uncle Foskitt said. Granny Tidd gave her a piercing stare.

Annie hurried on. "I went to Deepwater Neck and saw Captain Slew, and he's got a monstrous eel..." Annie blurted everything out, all in one breath.

"A monster eel? How big?" Uncle Foskitt's whiskers twitched angrily.

Annie nodded. "Almost as long as Tidd

Cottage, I'd say, and already big enough to tip a small craft over with a flick of its tail."

Uncle Foskitt thumped the table so hard that all the dishes flew up in the air. "Then something has to be done about that villain," he roared. "I won't stand it any longer. The water-folk will take action!"

He snatched at his jacket, and stormed to the door. "Granny Tidd, I'm a-going out. I may be some time." They heard his oars splash the water. "Blast you too, Billy Bantam, for bringing this trouble!" he yelled.

"Shall I see to the nets today?" asked Annie, sadly. "It wasn't Billy's fault at all. It was Billy that showed me what Slew was doing."

"Yes, my dear," sighed Granny Tidd. "You know, sometimes that Foskitt hasn't the right sort of wits in his head. Let's hope Billy Bantam knows it too."

Chapter Eight

The day was darkening, and Annie had visited as many nets as she could. As she rowed her haul of fish closer to Tidd Cottage, she heard Tilly crying and crying.

"Why couldn't I go in the boat?"

"Nobody went in my boat, chicken," said Annie, swinging her craft towards the mooring place.

"Not your boat. The beardy man's boat," Tilly sulked.

"Josh and Joe went in another boat? With a beardy man?"

"A big beardy man with ruby rings!" stated Tilly. "He wanted Uncle Foskitt, but he wasn't here, so he took the boys instead."

Annie stared aghast. Captain Slew had kidnapped the twins! Someone was cursing and shouting at the back of Tidd Cottage. Annie raced round, and saw an oar wedging an outhouse door shut. The old lady was locked in the lavvy!

Annie tugged away the oar, and out burst Granny Tidd, smoothing her skirts down furiously. She was in a rage.

"That daft 'un Foskitt! He weren't here when I needed him. He's still off trying to stir up folk against that big bully, the daft beanpole." Granny Tidd shook her head. "So Slew's took those two tiddly boys as hostages, that's what he's done, and likely enough he'll feed them to that eel."

"Surely not?" cried Annie, shocked, as Granny Tidd shooed them indoors like chickens, hugging them tightly. "Oh Annie, things is going from bad to worse!" she wept.

Night came on. Uncle Foskitt still wasn't back, so he didn't know the boys were missing. There was no way Annie could leave them on Uglow Slew's ship till dawn. She had to do something, and she'd need to have some help.

"I must go out, Granny Tidd," Annie said, going to the door.

"Aye. Do what you must, Annie," the old woman said, sighing softly, and hugging her ever tighter.

Annie waited on the bank. As the moon sailed across the sky, she saw the phantom, flickering like a candlelight between the dark stems of the reed beds. Annie took a deep breath, and called his name aloud.

"Bill? Billy? Billy Bantam?" The flickering light went out. "Billy, I have to get the boys back," she whispered into the darkness.

No phantom. Nothing. The air felt cold, as if chilled by Billy Bantam's anger.

Annie's heart sank. "I can't do it on my own," she shouted, lifting her hand in desperation. Why was Billy doing this to her, now? She recalled Uncle Foskitt's angry outburst: "Blast you too, Billy Bantam!" he'd yelled as he stormed off. No wonder Billy was silent.

"Listen, Billy, if you want folk like Foskitt to stop blaming you, you must show them the truth! Please! Come and help me, Billy."

Then she felt a breeze stir the rushes, and Billy was there. He raised a pale, glimmering hand in greeting, and they were on their way.

Chapter Nine

The boat swung out into the river, but the
current was against them, sweeping in from
the sea. Billy's face seemed lit by some
intense energy, like a cat. The little boat rose
and fell with the waves as Annie took it closer
to Slew's huge barrier. Silently they slid under
its shadow, and Annie tied the boat to a
rickety platform. The water was bubbling and
frothing where the eel writhed in its net.

Annie scrambled up a wooden ladder.
Lifting her head, inch by inch, she peered
along the untidy raft, between the ropes and
hooks and barrels. There, tied to a wooden
chest, were Josh and Joe, thumbs in their
mouths, and asleep. One of Slew's ruffians
lay nearby in a drunken stupor. Annie waited
a moment. She heard snores coming
from Slew's den. How could she
wake the boys, and not
start them crying?

She felt in her pocket. There, somewhat sticky, were Mam's boiled toffee-drops. Annie crept over, and hugged the boys. As they opened their eyes she winked and popped a toffee-drop into each mouth. They sucked, and smiled to see their sister.

"Sssh!" Annie whispered, pulling the knots undone. "Come on! Time to escape!"

"But not while I'm watching you!" Captain Uglow Slew was advancing towards them with a cutlass in his hand. He swished it swiftly to left and right. His one eye glinted cruelly, and his leering mouth was as red as fire. They had no chance at all.

Then something flickered beside the captain. Something tugged at his beard...

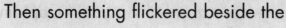

...and pulled at his hair.

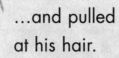

Something pinched his nose...

...and tugged at his ragbag robes.

It was Billy Bantam.

"Ouch!" Slew bellowed, "Get away from me, you flipping phantom!"

As he turned to fend Billy off, Annie's hand fixed around those sticky sweets in her pocket, scrunching them close together.

Silently she squeezed her fist hard, and hurled the clump of rock-hard toffee at Slew's one good eye. It hit like a cannonball, and he reeled round blindly.

At that very moment Annie yanked a rope that lay across the deck, catching Slew's feet, and down he smashed. He rolled across the wooden decking, howling and yelling.

The boys stared at Slew, and burst into giggles, but then an amazing thing happened. Their smile was reflected on Billy's face. Annie saw him throw his head back and laugh, and laugh. Yes, after all these years of loneliness, Billy Bantam was laughing again.

Annie hurried the boys off into the boat. But it was not all over.

"Annie, my dearie, we're here, we're here!"
shouted Uncle Foskitt.

A little fleet of boats and rafts and punts,
and all sorts of strange craft were heading
towards Slew's barrier, and the water-folk
were all shouting their anger.

Slew's crew charged out of the den and across the barrier as Captain Uglow Slew staggered to his feet, his face as red as an over-ripe plum.

"Aha!" he sneered, facing the angry boats. "Well, I've been waiting for this day, waiting for the worm to turn." He lifted his cutlass aloft. "'Cos I've got a worm that'll turn too. I've got my own slithery darling, and it'll do for the lot of you."

With a mighty yell, Slew slashed down, cutting the net loose. The water around the barricade seemed to bubble and boil, then a long ripple snaked over the shining surface. Up rose a cold, grey head, with gills like clustered seaweed around its neck. The thing stared around with cold, grey eyes.

"Get them!" Slew screamed his orders. "Get them, you worm!"

As the eel swirled and whirled about, everything else spun and twirled too. The wash lapped high along the banks, upsetting the nests of a dozen ducks, and tumbling water-rats out of their homes.

"What can I do?" groaned Uncle Foskitt.
"What can anyone do?"

Then, like a star shooting across the sky,
a glimmering light arched across the water
and landed on one of the huge pillars at the
mouth of the Neck. It was the Phantom of
Billy Bantam!

Chapter Ten

Billy stood there, glowing and brilliant beside
the broken lantern on the pillar. The mighty
eel swam towards him like a moth to a
flame. As the huge head rose up through
the foam, Billy Bantam knelt down. He put
out his hand, and the great eel paused.
Everyone saw Billy Bantam lean over and
stroke the eel's head. They heard his strange,
ghostly voice start to sing, over and over,
to the sad monstrous thing:

"Not cage, nor net,
Nor captivity,
Shall make you forget
The sea, the sea!
Shall make you forget
The SEA!"

As Billy's song died away, the eel's grey eyes grew steely, and the coils of its body wound and unwound.

"Be free, my friend! The sea is calling!" Billy murmured.

The mighty head sunk under the surface. For a moment Deepwater felt as if it was the centre of a whirlpool, where the water seemed as still as a sheet of glass. Then the river seemed to explode, and the eel was swimming, swimming through the waves, towards his captor, Uglow.

Suddenly the great eel struck with all its rage and power. Slew's crew were thrown in all directions, and the barricade was smashed to smithereens.

Hundreds of fragments were scattered across Deepwater Neck, and what was left sank below the surface. For a second, all was calm.

Then something rose among the flotsam, further along Deepwater Neck. It was the monstrous eel, but now it was dragging something in its mouth, something wearing a crusted coat and an old nightshirt, and a pair of old sea-boots.

"Stop, you overgrown worm! You're supposed to obey me..." The voice of Uglow Slew protested as the eel sped out into the freedom of the wide, wide sea. His voice kept growing weaker until it died away. At last the eel was just a dark squiggle on the horizon. Then it was gone.

The water-folk gasped. They looked up at the shining boy balanced on the pillar. Was this Billy, the one they'd been afraid of? No, this was Billy – the one who had saved them!

Uncle Foskitt's voice rang out, and then another, and another, louder and louder. "Hooray! Hooray for our own Billy Bantam! Hooray for our very own phantom!" they all cheered. "Bless you, Billy Bantam!"

The phantom boy stared around at the happy crowd. He shimmered and flickered, and gave a strange, pleased little smile. "Thank you, Annie!" he called, and disappeared.

"Thank you, Billy!" Annie called, safe with the twins in the little boat, "Thank *you!*"

Josh and Joe sat with their mouths wide open, gazing at the boy who'd help save them. The lantern light seemed to shine out of Deepwater for a moment. Then it fizzled and sparkled, and died away to darkness once more.

Chapter Eleven

Some days later Josh, Joe and Tilly were playing outside. They watched as the otter cubs swam and dived in the stream. They counted the frogs on the lily-pads. They saw the water vole struggling through the rushes. Suddenly a flock of birds shot up, calling and circling.

"Someone's coming," said Annie.

"Someone is," said Granny Tidd, thinking about the letter tucked in her pocket.

Annie strained her eyes to see. Could it be? She blinked, and looked again. A familiar figure came walking along the path. The boys leapt up, and raced towards her.

"Mam, Mam!" they cried. Tilly jumped up and ran towards her mother too.

Annie stood still. She felt muddled. Was Mam coming to collect them? Was she coming to take them away from Granny Tidd and Uncle Foskitt, away from the water and the sea and the wide sky?

"Hello, Granny Tidd," said Mam, shielding her eyes against the sun.

"Hello, my dear," said Granny Tidd, "Come in."

It was not until later, when the little ones were settled in their bed again, that Granny and Mam faced each other. "It's been good to have the children around us these past weeks," said Granny Tidd. She glanced over at Annie. "Especially this one."

"I'm sorry I've stayed away," said Mam. "This place reminded me so of their poor father –"

"That's the past, my dear," said Granny Tidd. "The children have a new life here now. Why not come and join them?"

Mam looked around. "It would be good," she sighed, "but I can't stay in Tidd Cottage," she added.

"Too many memories?" said Granny Tidd, and Mam nodded sadly. "Then I have an idea."

* * *

Billy watched.

White clouds scudded across the wide sky, and a bright banner waved cheerily above Deepwater Neck. Slew's old den was scrubbed and clean, outside and in.

The scent of fresh food drifted invitingly across the water. The door opened, and out came a tidy-looking woman in a clean white apron. Annie's Mam was carrying a basket full of crumbs. She tossed them on to the water, and a shriek of gulls descended, snatching the crusts.

Small craft sailed up and down the Neck, some on their way to the sea, some coming back into the rivers and streams criss-crossing the reedy land. There'd be plenty wanting dinner at his old haunt tonight, thought Billy.

Across the water, he spotted old Uncle
Foskitt bobbing in a small dinghy. Annie
came out of the door, clutching her
waterproof jacket.

"Come on then, child," said Uncle Foskitt.
"I'll be glad of your strong arms today."

Billy saw Annie take the oars, and watched
as the small boat slid off among the reeds.
Annie waved back at Mam, and smiled
happily. She peered over her shoulder. She
often thought she saw him, her phantom boy,
among the rushes.

Billy gazed after her for a moment, then
smiled happily too.

The Ghoul of
Bodger O'Toole

PENNY DOLAN

*It must have been
human once, but now it was
a ghostly, ghastly ghoul…*

SCHOLASTIC